**for Afra Amba and Noëlle Sage
and for their grandmother / great-grandaunt
Agnes Albertina**

SURINAME

SOUTH AMERICA

Printed in Belgium

First U.S. Edition   1 2 3 4 5 6 7 8 9 10

Library of Congress Cataloging in Publication Data was not available in time for publication of this book, but can be
obtained from the Library of Congress. I Lost My Arrow in a Kankan Tree. ISBN 0-688-12748-7. ISBN 0688-12749-5 (lib.).
Library of Congress Catalog Card Number 92-56102

I LOST MY ARROW
IN A KANKAN TREE

NONI LICHTVELD

LOTHROP, LEE & SHEPARD BOOKS   NEW YORK

Here in the forest, Jakóno lives with his mother and father and ten little brothers and sisters. Being the oldest, he hunts with his father for meat, but often there is not enough to go around.

One night Jakóno cannot sleep. "The forest gets smaller and smaller," he thinks, "while my family gets bigger and bigger. I had better go to town and find a job." And he sets off then and there.

He walks and he walks and he walks, until sunshine breaks between the leaves and birds begin to sing and animals awaken. "Odi odi—Good morning!" Jakóno calls to them all. "Today everyone is my friend!"

He finds some fruit for breakfast.

Then he notices a giant kankan tree. High in its branches sits a fat pigeon. Jakóno raises his bow and lets his arrow fly.

He is a good shot. The pigeon falls to the ground—a fine meal. But Jakóno's only arrow is lost, stuck high up in the kankan tree. There's nothing to be done about it now, so he packs up his pigeon and sets on his way again.

He walks and he walks and he walks, until he leaves the forest. There in the distance he sees a wisp of smoke. "A fire to cook my pigeon over," he thinks. On his way to the fire, he meets an old woman picking pumpkins. "Odi odi—Good day to you, Granmisi," Jakóno calls. "Do you need some help with those pumpkins?"

"Pumpkins!" the old woman snorts. "I am sick of pumpkins. If only I had something else to eat."

Jakóno pulls the pigeon from his sack. "For you," he says.

"Bless you, my boy." Granmisi beams. "Who are you and where have you come from?"

"I'm on my way to look for a job," Jakóno tells her. "When I shot this pigeon, I lost my arrow in the kankan tree. Now my pigeon stays with Granmisi....Hey, Granmisi, say, Granmisi, what will you give me?"

"I am poor and have little," says Granmisi. "Only this pumpkin can I give you."

"Thank you, Granmisi," says Jakóno, and he stuffs the pumpkin into his sack. Then he sets on his way again.

He walks and he walks and he walks, until he meets a man planing wood. With each stroke, he stuffs a handful of wood shavings into his mouth and gobbles them up.

"Odi odi—Good day to you, Carpenter," says Jakóno. "Why are you eating wood?"

"Haven't you heard?" says the carpenter. "A terrible famine has struck this place. Wood is all I have left to eat. Not very tasty, but better than nothing."

"Then take this pumpkin, Carpenter," says Jakóno. "It's much sweeter than wood."

"Heaven must have sent you!" cries the carpenter. "Who are you and where do you come from?"

Jakóno tells his tale:
"I lost my arrow in a kankan tree.
The kankan tree gave me his pigeon,
my pigeon stayed with Granmisi,
Granmisi gave me her pumpkin,
my pumpkin now stays with the carpenter....
Hey, Carpenter, say, Carpenter,
what will you give me?"

   "I've nothing to give you
except this walking stick,"
says the carpenter.

   "Thank you," says Jakóno,
and he sets on his way again.

He walks and he walks and he walks, until he comes upon some fruit trees. "This stick is very useful," he thinks, but before he has taken three bites from his fruit, he is startled by an old man yelling.

"You stupid beasts!" the man screams.

"What are you doing?" Jakóno calls out.

"I must get these cows to the meadow," the old man wails. "But if one moves a leg forward, the other moves two legs backward. I am beat!"

"Don't give up yet, Cowman," says Jakóno. "I have just the thing for you." And he hands the cowman his stick.

Hop! Hop! The cows leap over the ditch. "Bless you, my boy," says the cowman. "Who are you and where do you come from?"

So Jakóno tells his tale again:
"I lost my arrow in a kankan tree.
The kankan tree gave me his pigeon,
my pigeon stayed with Granmisi,
Granmisi gave me her pumpkin,
my pumpkin stayed with the carpenter,
the carpenter gave me his stick,
my stick now stays with the cowman....
Hey, Cowman, say, Cowman,
what will you give me?"

    "How about some milk?" says the cowman.
"It will quench your thirst on your journey."

    "Thank you, Cowman," says Jakóno,
and he sets on his way again.

He walks and he walks and he walks, until he meets a man digging in a ditch, then drinking muddy water.
"What on earth are you doing?" Jakóno asks.

"Haven't you heard?" says the mud digger. "It hasn't rained around here for years, so I'm digging for muddy water. Not very tasty, but at least it's wet."

"Muddy water could make you very sick," says Jakóno. "You had better take this." And he gives the mud digger his milk.

"Heaven has sent you my way!" cries the mud digger. "Who are you and where do you come from?"

So Jakóno tells his tale again:
"I lost my arrow in a kankan tree.
The kankan tree gave me his pigeon,
my pigeon stayed with Granmisi,
Granmisi gave me her pumpkin,
my pumpkin stayed with the carpenter,
the carpenter gave me his stick,
my stick stayed with the cowman,
The cowman gave me his milk,
my milk now stays with the mud digger....
Hey, Mud Digger, say Mud Digger,
what will you give me?"

"All I have is this old wheelbarrow," says the mud digger. "Take it please, and good luck to you!"

"Thank you, Mud Digger," says Jakóno, and he sets on his way again.

He walks and he walks and he walks, until he is worn out. At last he puts down his wheelbarrow and settles into it to sleep. But who is this strange man he sees now?

"Boy, I am a poor prisoner," says the man. "My punishment is to roll these stones, back and forth, from here to there, from there to here, today and tomorrow and tomorrow. My back is about to break."

"I have something to make your life easier," Jakóno tells him, and he gives the prisoner his wheelbarrow.

"You have saved my back!" the prisoner cries. "Who are you and where do you come from?"

So Jakóno tells his tale again:
"I lost my arrow in a kankan tree.
The kankan tree gave me his pigeon,
my pigeon stayed with Granmisi,
Granmisi gave me her pumpkin,
my pumpkin stayed with the carpenter,
the carpenter gave me his stick,
my stick stayed with the cowman,
the cowman gave me his milk,
my milk stayed with the mud digger,
the mud digger gave me his wheelbarrow,
my wheelbarrow now stays with the prisoner....
Hey, Prisoner, say, Prisoner,
what will you give me?"

The prisoner thinks for a moment. Then he ducks between two boulders and returns with a sack of gold. "I've no use for this out here," he says. "Take it please, and good luck to you."

"Thank you, Prisoner," says Jakóno, and he sets on his way again.

He walks and he walks and he walks,
until he reaches the town gate. "Odi
odi—Good evening," he calls to the
townspeople. "Can anyone tell me
where I might find a job?"

"A job!" say the people all at once.
"Listen, boy. This country is poor.
The king's treasury is empty of gold.
He can't even afford a wedding for
his daughter. Even the trash cans
are empty! And you ask about a
job. Ridiculous!"

"Then can anyone tell me where the king's palace is?" Jakóno asks, and the townspeople point him down the street.

Jakóno knocks on the palace door.

"Who are you and what do you want?" asks a gruff guard.

"I want to see the king," Jakóno answers. "I have the answer to his problem."

"You'll have to see the grand vizier first," says the guard.

"Can you really solve the king's problem?" asks the grand vizier.

Jakóno smiles but does not say a word.

"There's nothing to smile about," the grand vizier warns. "Beware not to fool with us, boy, or you'll be a prisoner pushing stones! Now follow me to the king."

Jakóno bows low before the unhappy king and holds out his bag of gold. "Here is the answer to your problem," he says.

The king is wild with joy. Four times he dances around his throne, and each time round he embraces Jakóno. "Who are you and where do you come from?" he finally asks.

So Jakóno tells his tale again:
"I lost my arrow in a kankan tree.
The kankan tree gave me his pigeon,
my pigeon stayed with Granmisi,
Granmisi gave me her pumpkin,
my pumpkin stayed with the carpenter,
the carpenter gave me his stick,
my stick stayed with the cowman,
the cowman gave me his milk,
my milk stayed with the mud digger,
the mud digger gave me his wheelbarrow,
my wheelbarrow stayed with the prisoner,
the prisoner gave me his gold,
my gold now stays with the king....
Hey, King, say, King,
what will you give me?"

"A good piece of land for you to farm," says the king, "and I'll throw in a donkey and a cart. Take them, please, and thank you. At last my daughter can marry!"

So Jakóno rides home in his new donkey cart.
His family is overjoyed to see him return.
"Where have you been?" they all want to know.
"And what have you been doing?"
So Jakóno tells his tale once more:
"I lost my arrow in a kankan tree.
The kankan tree gave me his pigeon,
my pigeon stayed with Granmisi,
Granmisi gave me her pumpkin,
my pumpkin stayed with the carpenter,
the carpenter gave me his stick,
my stick stayed with the cowman,
the cowman gave me his milk,
my milk stayed with the mud digger,
the mud digger gave me his wheelbarrow,
my wheelbarrow stayed with the prisoner,
the prisoner gave me his gold,
my gold stayed with the king,
the king gave me a donkey and a cart
and a good piece of land for us to farm,
so we'll never be hungry again!"